DEATH OF THE SPIDER

DEATH OF THE SPIDER

Michèle Mailhot

Translated by Neil B. Bishop
with a preface by
Marie-Claire Blais

Talonbooks • Vancouver • 1991

copyright © 1991 Michèle Mailhot

preface © 1991 Marie-Claire Blais

translations © 1991 Neil B. Bishop

published with the assistance of the Canada Council

Talonbooks
201/1019 East Cordova Street
Vancouver, British Columbia
Canada, V6A 1M8

Designed and typeset in Leawood by Pièce de Résistance Ltée.
Printed and bound in Canada by Hignell Printing Ltd.

Printed in Canada.

First printing: September 1991.

Canadian Cataloguing in Publication Data

Mailhot, Michèle.
  (Mort de l'araignée. English)
  Death of the spider

  Translation of: La mort de l'araignée.
  ISBN 0-88922-298-3

  I. Title. II. Title: Mort de l'araignée. English.
PS8526.A49M613 1991   C843'.54   C91-091550-4
PQ3919.2.M34M613 1991

Preface

Michèle Mailhot, an author of considerable importance thanks to her eight novels and two volume diary, has until now been known to English-speaking readers only through her *Coming of Age (Veuillez agréer . . .)*, an austere yet admirably powerful novel translated by David Lobdell. Quebec authors are familiar with David Lobdell's sensitive and respectful attitude towards them and their work, and they know he saw translation as a richly subtle, demanding art. David passed away some months ago, and that grievous loss will forever prevent any of us, his writer and reader friends, from discovering the intuitive understanding, the poignant simplicity with which he would have translated *Le Portique*, a Michèle Mailhot novel he was planning to work on this year. He told me that he greatly admired both Michèle's intellectual courage and the quality of her style. Then, true to his scruples and modesty when faced with a work such as Michèle's *Béatrice vue d'en bas* (Boréal, 1989), he felt only a poet could translate from French to English its prodigious abundance of words and topsy-turvy poetic expressions, its puns displaying with full freedom (*Béatrice* is, along with the much earlier *Le Fou de la reine*, among Michèle Mailhot's most fully free books) their ironic charm and cruelty — for this novel, like Gunther Grass' *The Tin Drum*, is about a child who observes the world, and society. "Vue d'en bas" ("Seen from below"), that society is a cold, abuse-filled hell in which the humiliated child, already a Rimbaud-like prodigy, seeks warmth in the heat of her own words and so finds a first consolation for the wounds of love.

With the same modesty and audacious tenacity as David Lobdell, Neil Bishop has translated another challenging work — challenging, and how very prophetic when one learns to decipher its signs whose meaning becomes inescapable on close reading, for suddenly they lay bare the raw, flagrant injustice that scars women from birth, in a detailed, scathing, sometimes nightmarish depiction, utterly real and realistic, of the limitless oppression that crushes a woman both in her private life, with her husband and children, and when she is lost among a group of other women, in the midst of what one might call a "flock", gliding, mute, towards the slaughterhouse, the gradual and total extinction of its freedom. Neil Bishop has unhesitatingly revived this novel, *Death of the Spider*, in the true light of its prophecy (be it but dreamed), in the bright light too of its modernism, for this novel is both a poetic indictment of our contemporary society and a forerunner of the feminist novel — while admirably avoiding the traps of theory and rigidity. The author draws us into our very depths, our own submissiveness, our own hereditary sheep-like docility, she shuts us in with her main character, staring at the spider on the ceiling, in that secret bedroom of rebellion where this nameless heroine has withdrawn to think about her fate which is also ours and where she and we are left, alone with the shameful images of our own condition, our own, often willing, bondage. Michèle Mailhot also leaves us with the overflow from her imaginary screen whose words have become transpiercing images of our everyday lives, images which, even when covered in, or translucent with, those sensuous glows our poor dreams so gladly don, nonetheless cling to a precise, gripping, raw reality. So it is the priest (whatever guise he takes in the dream) who orders the young woman to "go forth and multiply", while the spider (or the man who would crush her freedom, as the Pope can be heard even now telling women they must bear children) examines, probes, the woman's body. And towards each one of the figures of male oppression — priest, doctor, ruler — marches the flock: Mireille and her sisters. Sometimes there is a wayside pause for pleasure or tenderness with husband or lover, but such pauses are pervaded by an ever-lingering shadow, worry, or even lurking ferocity. Woman is never untroubled, nor left to her own peace, to the contemplation of a space truly her own. The child is the sole wonder, for whose tears "flowers spring", but whose sunny presence soon leaves us; isn't that him, already grown, lying on the chesterfield, smoking, distant, lost in those toxic dreams that our culture offers, idleness and the stupor of drugs in lieu of a healthy, viable future? And besides, while Philippe is love and pleasure, he is also the warrior world which must be kept at bay, he is also the judge who threatens to expell all these women from the court, "Order, order!", he shouts. And when Philippe claims that "childbirth is not an illness" and that it therefore entails no pain, and that the woman should just shut up, the judge and the priest cry out, "They are possessed! How can they still shout when they've been gagged!" Then comes the painful image of "hundreds of newborns on the flagstones". And these images grip us in a stranglehold, because we can sense — even if Michèle Mailhot scorns the clumsiness of everyday language by using an unsettling, iconoclastic idiom like that of dreams and especially of bad dreams — we sense everywhere, in this frescoe molded from our very flesh, how much these scenes possess their own order and have a place in the reality of our lives. Neil Bishop has understood this novel's urgency and despair, its intelligent, creative despair, for it reveals a glimpse of hope for solidarity between the sexes, at the end of the tunnel where the spider is dying of its passive submissiveness. Hope there is, for Mireille and her sisters have thrown off their yoke; a few captives have already fled towards life, where they have lit their warning signals, and their hearths.

Readers will be grateful indeed to Neil Bishop and to Talon Books for making this powerful, beautiful, uncompromising, challenging novel available to the English-speaking public.

Marie-Claire Blais

To My Children

Death of the Spider

My family and friends think I am on a flight that took off this morning for London. They are all relieved, especially Philippe, who hopes this temporary separation will rid me forever of all thought of a permanent one, such travel therapy having worked four times. That was the trap to avoid, the risk not to run. Having resold the plane ticket, I decided to rent a room.

How long have I stayed in this room? Five, ten, twenty days? It hardly matters, since in a way I have spent my whole life here. Mireille used to live in the same building. She was in a room facing south, across from the park. A tiny, sun-filled room. Tree shadows danced on its walls and played nonchalantly in its unbelievable disorder: books, clothes, empty bottles, dried flowers, suitcases, cardboard boxes, glasses, chandeliers, on the bed, the table, the chiffonier and the floor, everywhere objects indispensable to her dreams, her life, and thrown down just anywhere, as in her life. I liked that room which so resembled her. I had come a few times and Mireille, bustling about nervously, had immediately tried to tidy things up a bit, exactly as she did with her ideas when we talked. Soul and room filled with warm sunshine and equally cluttered. So when Mireille cleared a space for me on the armchair, I would smile a bit, and she knew why. Piqued, she would throw back her long hair, revealing her face, take a cigarette and look frantically for unfindable matches. I used to laugh out loud, and she felt like crying. I had to come close, hold her head against me, call her "Douce," "Douce," gently, to stop the jostling shadows hounded by my laugh. She would slowly calm down as I spoke to her, leading her into my underground depths, where she brought her sun. Its light illuminated a mysterious, rigid, order fixed in terribly cold tunnels whose walls, made of sharp rectangles, oozed ice-cold water, as though a spring were trapped behind them.

Mireille had come with me so often and so deep into my catacombs, with such courage and such patience, she so graceful, slender and long as an arrow shot into the sun, that, quite naturally, it was to her that I turned when I wanted to be alone.

The rest of the house belonged to a completely different world. The same old ladies had been hanging on for five or ten years, shut in, cloistered, forgotten, mute, getting along with each other just well enough to be able to share kitchen and bathroom without clashing. Since the slightest personal casualness threatened to spur the others to invasive liberties, intransigent self-discipline had become the rule indicating to all the limits of strict communal decency. One did not suffocate in this house: breathing itself had been decelerated.

How had Mireille, who always moved like a tornado, doors slamming in her blasts, come to be accepted, then cherished by these old, soft-treading ladies? Thanks to her youth, without a doubt: a gust of fresh air in their mouldy, walled-up lives, a sonorous gesture piercing their silence, a vibrant presence that would dust off memories and restore their lost, smiling colours. The tenants would come, one after the other, to bring her phone messages, cakes, show her pictures, and talk to her of this once lively, luxurious, festive house. I liked that unexpected Mireille, attentive to these women, forgetting herself - that was the image of her I remembered when I rang at her door: an old lady, to talk to her, stretching up like a stump proud of its past, while the long girl, to listen, bent in a graceful, supple, tender curve, like a young birch.

I had not seen Mireille for two months but it was as though I had left her the day before. Our friendship had a mysterious, troubling yet comforting continuity. I knew where she was and how she felt, but, for all sorts of reasons that made less sense with each meeting, I hesitated to join her. My stiffness was gradually softened by her confidence which I at first had judged to be foolhardy and excessive, too much like her character, that of an angry, violent, worried, selfish child, seemingly so very free, but prisoner of an impatient, proud, anguished dream, tenacious still but increasingly worried as beings and things around yielded while her dream did not budge, producing nothing, except time lost.

No doubt she used to stop near me just another minute to marvel once again at the effect of her charm, which fed but never satisfied her. So I found her enthusiastic confidence was more worrying than reassuring. Did I seek to see it as something other than a fleeting gentleness, a tender moment suspended in our rushing lives? I did not ask myself that question, but it is strange that I was certain I must go there, and nowhere else. Mireille at once rented the only room to let in the building, and the landlady gave her the keys without my even having to appear.

I opened the door onto a vast abyss. A black smell, shut up in there for an eternity, fell on me like a stinking trap. Recovering my self-control, I reached for the light switch, but Mireille at once intervened and lit a standard lamp whose subdued light let one observe without really seeing, protecting me from the ugliness left in the shadows and capable of killing you outright if it jumped out all at once, as I realized later.

I saw the bare bed first, the blue striped mattress and the pillows stiff as grey stones. "I'll go get some blankets." Her voice seemed unreal, otherworldly; I felt I was hearing it for the first time, and that from far off, somewhere on the sun, outside this hole, marvelous music was reaching me, carried by some strange echo.

I set down my suitcase and stood motionless, focussing on the slowly forming shadows. Venetian blinds covered the entire right wall. Raising them amidst a dust-storm, I discovered two enormous, soot-black windows, barricaded with iron bars rounded into a basin. Why bars? Aggression from without was inconceivable, as the third-floor room overlooked a closed courtyard, a kind of grey tube cemented on its five sides and opening onto a sky too distant to be seen even if I stretched my neck. To savour my freedom, I had chosen a prison.

I forgot to look at the ceiling, it was so high and lost in shadow. Anyway, the rest of the room was enough to hold my full attention. How could anyone have made a room so horrible? Only a deliberate desire for ugliness, determination to create the repulsive, could explain such extraordinary success. I was convinced that someone had wished this room to be ghastly and that it was not rented out because they had not wanted to rent it. But why? My imagination went wild.

I could still return the key, look for something different elsewhere. But I was fascinated by the pure ugliness of this cubbyhole. Any reality that attains a summit, be it of beauty or ugliness, loathsomeness or attractiveness, gentleness or cruelty, takes full hold of my being: I can no longer move, nor even think. That reality lives in my stead, and in me, and expresses itself in dire suffering, as though my soul wanted to shatter for having become *that*. I can but suffer the gentle or terrible torture of its existing through me. I am the handicapped, the tree, the wounded, the beautiful, the macabre.

I am this room which has invaded me; and its details, gradually emerging from the shadows, enter in their turn, pile up, furnish me - a chocolate brown desk, a big, stiff cardboard cupboard in lieu of a wardrobe, a plastic-covered chiffonier supporting a cut-glass shadeless lamp, a green leatherette armchair with chrome arms, the sort you see in waiting rooms, a headless bed, an orangish arborite table near a crippled torchère lamp and two varnished folding chairs. All that on grey linoleum where big red flowers were squashed like dried blood. Thick soot everywhere, the residue of incinerated bodies, blown here by an invisible mouth. I was dumbfounded. The ceiling lamp suddenly came on. The shock of the light wrenched the room away from me and scattered it into

insignificant bits. Ugliness turned into the simply banal, inoffensive in this cutting brightness. Now it was up to me to live in this room.
What was I going to do? Where to start? I lay down on the bed so as to let the emotions experienced since that morning settle and to recover at least some notion of peace. My eyes bulged as I opened my mouth in a silent scream - a monstrous spider was hanging just above my head, enormous, hairy, grey. In a split second, just time enough to see it clearly in all its repugnant horror, it dove headlong into me!

I began to exist differently, weaving the threads of an immense web around someone resembling me and flowing, gliding in space like a dragonfly with its sudden retreats, its unpredictable stops, its jerky yet fluid dance sketching the invisible lines of its mysterious destiny. I saw it here, it was already there, fleeting, elusive, stopped, off again, here again, elsewhere, gracefully daft, while the spider slowly designed the pattern of encounter.

Spider and dragonfly, observer and observed, I doubled myself without splitting by moving between the threads of an elastic, mobile canvas framing successive, rapid scenes of extraordinary precision. I would advance a "leg," and the image at once disappeared, to reappear a little further on, transformed, hemmed into a net that surrounded but could not hold it. The invisible canvas covered the entire ceiling and I could sense it only by the images appearing here and there, in its rectangles, like little luminous screens. Funny images, sad, comical, sharp and fuzzy ones, in jerks, in fadeout, superimposed, a real jumbled film, its strangeness seeming quite natural to me, as in a dream whose incoherence never disconcerts us. So the mixed-up images followed one another in a secret rhythm whose very abruptness and tone changes followed a harmonious line revealed only by the continuity of my emotion. I was lucid however, I could clearly see this spider-like chandelier, a shabby, dusty, grey, crystal chandelier with electric bulbs at the end of its legs and twisted wires coming out of its open stomach where members had been torn off. It was still pretending to be a spider but I knew it was acting, that it was not a real spider. Because the real spider is under the wharf.

    I am sitting on the wharf, my feet in the water, I'm four, and watching a dragonfly stopped above the lake, then right by my hand. The spider slowly comes out from among the wooden planks, enormous, and heads for my fingers. With my other hand, I grab my sandal and smash it down onto that horror, it squirts into a little sawdust mixed with a whitish liquid. I jump into the water, swim, I'm far, swimming, Mommy can't see me, no one sees me, I don't want to return to shore and the spiders, I flee, I'd rather drown. Fingers fumble in my mouth, my throat, I vomit muck. Mother is covered with mud; I am frightened: the spider! They wash me, they cuddle me, they console me, I'm totally soft, relaxed in their nets, abandoned. I'm ready to let them devour me but it is time for mass, and off they all go to church.

    The huge, empty church smells of candles, incense, gentleness. I am talking to God, I am talking to my sole self, I'm tired of being alone, I say He *should* exist because that would be so convenient: I could bawl him out, tell Him that I don't understand anything, but that I agree, that I haven't the strength to adjust to His world of madmen, that I am leaving, that I abandon myself to His most holy wretched will. I am old, I'm forty, I've gone all round my garden, I'm bored. I pull out this last plant, an ivy that twists me up in quiet suffocation. When they throw stones at me over the wall, I take them and build cenotaphs in this garden of the dead. I am neither joyful nor sad, like a gravedigger-monk preparing the tomb of his beloved brethren and worrying nonetheless: who will bury me, since I shall die last? Children's voices rattle the wall, pierce it, and a whole section crumbles, burying me harmlessly. I can hear the children playing overhead and shouting delightedly: "The spiders are coming out!" I feel I'm going to die and I try to advise God of this important event. But God hasn't time to listen to me: he is discussing the indissolubility of marriage with the council of bishops. I get angry and walk stark naked into the august assembly. Indignant, all the men get up, except one who looks like Philippe and is masturbating; they rush towards me, some to pierce me with their crosiers, others to cover me with their copes. I decide to give birth right there. Out of respect, they kneel, petrify, and disintegrate into grey sand. Bishop Philippe has volatalized and Mireille is sitting in the seat he left empty. I am very happy she is there, and show her the child: she takes it and carries it off with her. A man wearing a cassock enters the Sistine Chapel and asks me: "What have you done with your child? And why are you dressed like a man?" I raise my eyes to the Creator sitting on the ceiling and protest I was naked on arrival. Hell laughs, heaven fulminates, they make a frightful din. A voice behind a wall calls "Mommy"; I try to get out but stumble against all the doors. Philippe then appears holding his member in his hands like a fiery sword, he opens the door and says "I exile you from Paradise." I slip out quickly, and the whole building collapses behind me.

Mireille has decided to flee our concentration camp the very next night, alone if she has to. I beg her to wait, I show her my map, the slightly longer but absolutely safe road by which we shall escape. She doesn't listen, and pummels me with her fists. "*You're* the one holding me prisoner." My feet are in chains and she does not see them. Then I hear her shouting from the river that runs below the prison. It's night. She's screaming "Help!" I quickly leave by the hole I had begun to dig, just as I see her swept away by the flow of muddy water. Finally I arrive outside, in a desert. No one around except Philippe, holding a bayonet and aiming at me from atop a watchtower. I wait for him to kill me. He shouts, "I'm protecting you." From what? From whom? I see nothing but white sand. Mireille climbs the watchtower ladder. He does not turn around, watches me, still pointing his weapon at me, a strange smile on his lips. Mireille slips between him and me and faces him. She kisses him and he inserts his bayonet between her thighs. She laughs, moans, then, at the same time as she cries out in climax, a bomb explodes under the watchtower, which rises skywards like a rocket. The blond desert is burned. My throat too. Mireille has drowned and I'm dying of thirst.

Hiding behind a clump of bushes, I am watching

the house I live in across the street. How ugly it is from outside! Someone walks by and tells me I'm right to hide, I'm so ugly. How can I explain to him that's not why I'm hiding? Just then, the front of my house falls down like a panel and you can see all the rooms, even those in the back. Everything is lovely, clear, clean: the immense fireplace in the living room, the kitchen with its red bricks and dutch tiles, the big wooden staircase, our blue bedroom... I am preparing the meal and crying. The children come home, ignore me, eat, argue. The elder asks "Where's mother?" I answer "You know she's travelling." "Good, we can have fun." He is half-lying on a deep chesterfield in a lethargically moving oriental decor: palm branches, music, incense glide, mingle, meld. A veiled woman pedicures his toenails, another lights a long pipe for him while a man massages his thighs and stomach. "I don't know if Mommy is having such a lovely trip," he murmurs. The room next door, from which I can see him, is full of women. I ask them what they are doing there: "We are waiting for him to send for us," answers one. Mireille approaches and draws me to her. I struggle like I'm crazy, I bite the wrought arabesques of the door, I want to go slap my son. Then they call me. But suddenly my legs go so weak, and my stomach gets so warm, that I can scarcely move. They gently push me. I both fear and hope he recognizes me. But when I draw near, it is no longer him but an enormous, greasy pacha, a mountain of lechery who lays me down on him. He uses me like a rag doll, turning me over and over, scolding me, caressing me, penetrating and filling me. My whole body orgasms, my wounds bleed a warm liquid, I melt into absolute bliss and faint with pleasure.

The lawyer's secretary invites me to be seated. "The lawyer will see you in a few minutes." In this antechamber which looks exactly like a presbytery office, I feel comfortable, relaxed, even though I might well be in for a long wait because of the people in the lineup: these people are coming out of another room where a white haired man in a soutane has them sign papers while he makes the sign of the cross. He is drowning in work, gesticulating, blessing, blessing endlessly, and giving certificates to children as he says "Multiply!" There are already enough people, it seems to me, and I begin to get impatient. I shall surely not be liberated before dawn. The lawyer recognizes me and invites me to enter his office. "I'm not in such a rush," I answer. "Oh yes, but yes, you are in a rush, and so am I." Dressed like a horseback rider, shoulders thrown back, he is sure of himself and his strength. We are mounted on two superb palominos, in a mad ride, he is in front, laughing riotously, and I am scared to death. He rides on ahead and disappears. My horse gets excited, throws me to the ground and heads back to the stable. I am alone in an unfamiliar place and my legs are paralyzed. A donkey passes close by: I remember seeing it in the stable, near my palomino. When I call it, it pricks up its long ears and laughs with all its teeth while pursuing its lazy walk. This donkey looks like someone I know; Philippe again? No, that's impossible, Philippe is not a donkey. "And why" asks the donkey huffily, "should I not be deemed worthy of being Philippe?" I explain that he is off the topic, that the dignity of certain beings is not necessarily that of others, that there are dignified donkeys and undignified men, and vice versa.

Then the judge gives a great blow with his hammer and demands silence. The whole audience awaits my sentence after the muddled indictment I have just stammered out.

"How dare you appear before me stark naked?"

"But your honour, I was just born!"

"At forty years of age?"

"Yes, at forty."

The judge shrugs, dejected, scratches his head: the criminal code did not make provision for the crime of late birth. A dove, seemingly knowledgeable on the topic of obscure birth, lands on his head and inspires therein this luminous sentence:

"I condemn you to live."

My children rush up and hug me, my grandmother and mother leave, tight-lipped. The lawyer is parading on his stallion. All this racket suddenly stops. I am alone, I know not where, nor why, draped in anguish as in a great lead cape, the weight of all these bellies through which I must travel to give birth to myself.

Without touching the ground I walk in some arid land. I come from nowhere and am going nowhere. Emptiness around. I reach for unreal objects that disappear just as I am about to touch them. Before me, abysses full of memories: what step could I make that would not send me tumbling into them? Illusion again: there is nothing in front of me except me in front of nothing and quite amazed not to have been swallowed up. Am I advancing?

No, I am in suspension. An intolerable but extraordinary sensation: I am touching nothingness, I am not seized and I seize not. Present? Yes. Absent? Yes. I have even forgotten to breathe. How long can one live without breathing? The question does not upset me any more than if I were asking the time. I know one can spend a lifetime without breathing, so I am not worried in the slightest. The mysterious place suddenly changes into an immense kitchen, in a hospital or prison, I don't know which. Several women, bent over enormous pots, greedily breathe in the steam coming from them. Their stubborn faces seem tired. I try to open the windows but there aren't any and the acrid odour is poisoning the atmosphere more and more. I vainly try to tear them away from these harmful vapours, I want to flee and to convince them to follow me, but they stubbornly stay stuck where they are. A skinny one clinging to her ladle assures me she will not die if she breathes in the odour of the soup. I lean over her dirty pot: simmering bones, and I am sure they are human. "Cannibals!", I shout. "You're crazy," replies the spoon lady. "I am getting dinner ready for my children." A sorcerer disguised as a cook is drumming on an upside-down cauldron. "Dinner's ready, dinner's ready." Then hundreds of children come out of the pots, jump on the women and gobble them up. Philippe arrives for dinner and bellows because the children have not left him any apple pie. I remind him that he was not expected home for dinner. "So what," says he, "you should always wait for the master to arrive." I begin to cook thousands of pies and, as soon as they are ready, they disappear into a voracious system of soft tubes. My mother, a little further on, is doing the same work. When my daughter offers to come and help me, I blow up the ghastly, gut-filled machine. She cries, but from each tear that falls springs up a daisy. I weave them into a garland for her and she walks majestically on the unknown sea which has appeared out of nowhere, just for her.

My secretary comes out of my office and locks the door. The room is spacious, impressive. I am certainly at the head of a thriving company, as this discreet luxury proves. Documents, filing cabinets, files surround me. The very keen feeling of my importance is nonetheless mitigated by an unpleasant sensation I cannot identify. A long list of telephone calls to make to Moscow, Mexico and Paris, a bundle of cheques to sign, a pile of letters post-marked from around the world are waiting for me to deign tend to them. Let them wait, my power allows me to take as long as I like. I sprawl my feet out on my desk, as all real bosses have a knack for; but the strange uneasiness persists. When the intercom announces that the Pope wishes to speak to me, I get angry: did I not tell him that I would talk to Jesus Christ and not to his secretary? My secretary reminds me that Jesus does not speak French. "I know, I read his last letter, full of mistakes. And what about the gift of tongues? Correct that letter and send it back to him, mentioning the total immersion method. But politely: he's still influential. And don't put through a single call, I'm busy."

I take out my knitting and, with two forks as needles, I make an endless scarf. Philippe's secretary informs me he will not be coming for dinner, since an urgent meeting has been called by the union whose delegation I lead without stopping my knitting. Philippe refuses to negotiate under such circumstances, and everyone approves. I undo the knitting, resign, and leave the meeting. A nun greets me: "You have made the right decision," and disappears after giving me a little box. I open it. It is empty.

In a prison cell, I am sitting on a swing, my feet unable to touch the ground. They are probably punishing me for never having liked swings: even as a tiny little girl this game made me as banaly sick as, in books, it poetically uplifted the muslin dresses of exemplary little girls. I try again to play the game, to experience the pretty picture of good little girls borne skywards, even if I know how much my physical inability to swing goes hand in hand with my profound contempt for these false, hedgehopping take-offs that propel the dreamer ever farther backwards and make her look less like a beautiful bird than a stupid pendulum. Since I can justify my contempt so reasonably, why go on with this game? Then I understand that I am not allowed to get off, nor to remain motionless: I am condemned to swing, and do so. With each oscillation a whistling comes from the ceiling where I can see the ingenious process of my execution. The rigid ropes of the swing, when they are at an angle, open two valves that release a pressurized poisonous gas. I cannot help swinging and hearing the gas whistling my death. My mother, facing me, exhorts me to resignation and courage. When the swing approaches her I stretch out my hand:

she removes one of my many rings and pushes the swing. I start crying, but not once do I think of shouting, jumping off or stopping the infernal mechanism. I feel I have finally become a real good little girl. I am pleasing Mommy and am going to heaven to join the angels in muslin dresses.

This is at least the twentieth time I have taken this road climbing a huge mountain. My inability to scale it remains total and as I approach I know how the mountain is going to escape me: my car is going the limit, I'm climbing, climbing, and as I approach the peak the road becomes vertical. The wheels no longer grip the pavement and the car tumbles into the abyss behind. Despite numerous failed attempts, I keep taking this road even though I fear the chasm that may lurk on the other side. Here I am half-way up, the slope increases, balance is hanging by a thread. I floor it and, for the first time, I reach the top where my mother greets me, takes my hand and shows me, on the other slope, a long, wide stairway descending towards a sumptuous green valley. How did my mother get here? I left her a moment ago, taking care of my sick brother. Relatives were waiting for me and wanted to prevent me from leaving, abandoning them in such dire straights. "The dead must bury the dead," said I, jumping into my car speeding towards my suicide mountain, whose gentle green slopes I can finally admire. When I start building a shelter on it, I realize that all the material is back at the house to which I do not want to return for fear I shall never be able to climb back up the terrible slope. Looking backwards, I no longer see the chasm: the

mountain peak gently slides away in all directions and I can build my house anywhere, since everything necessary is here, within reach of hand, of tenderness.
What's that? A house? A barn? Room after room, dark, full of people having a good time with smoke, alcohol and hands. I move ceaselessly among them, looking for my torn-off arm. Have you seen Mireille walking around arm in arm with my arm, without me on the end of my arm? No one seems to notice I am one-armed. "Why have you got two glasses?" someone asks me. "You're drinking way too much! A glass in each hand!" They laugh. "I've got two glasses to help me forget I've lost a hand." They laugh even louder. The telephone rings: it's Mireille, and I have to shout my head off because of the noise of the crowd: "Come back, I'm all alone." Mireille does not believe me, with good reason. I want to explain the situation to her but I hear her fall silent and judge me. As soon as the call is cut off, everyone falls silent and we go and kneel before a Hindu goddess with dozens of motionless arms, frozen in perfection. "Don't budge!" shouts the photographer, "I want the perfect picture!" When I learn he is taking pictures for funeral cards, I rush up, grab the camera and smash it to bits that immediately become birds. "The souls! The souls!" shouts the photographer, "What have you done?" You know I can't photograph souls."
"Then you shouldn't photograph anything at all," I tell him.
The goddess waves her hands as I fly off over the others, slowly, blessedly, blissfully, in a long glide.

What a strange idea to have built my house here! I have to walk forever, take a boat, cross a river that threatens to sweep me away in its tormented waters, climb a steep hill, slippery on this rainy day. And, after having come so far, in lieu of a house I find a simple platform, dizzyingly high, exposed to the four winds, with my bed placed not in the reassuring centre but just on the edge, right by the abyss. Although I am dissatisfied with the place, I am unable to go elsewhere because the platform has been hoisted as high as possible, without any visible link to the ground. Down there a publisher's wife is strolling naked in the sun, holding a glass of cognac, free as the wind, bewitching. She puts me to bed, consoles me (I know not why), embraces me, pirouettes, sings, dances with marvellous ease of limb and mind. I notice that people, including her husband, are watching her, and I so inform her. That doubles her gaiety, it must be more a case of exhibitionism than of that spontaneity I was so pleased to see and that reassured me despite the precarious balance of our platform. My disappointment reminds me that I have an appointment with Mireille. This other woman's false grace, amiability and affection suddenly disgust me as much as they had seemed comforting a little earlier. Then her husband lands like a crow and orders me to write before leaving. The very idea seems crazy to me in such a situation; however, a man is sitting there at the table, both feet dangling in the abyss, his eyes shaded by a visor, tirelessly blackening innumerable pages promptly gone with the wind. I tell the publisher that I have written everything, the proof is that I too can fly, which I do, with the pages, and with the same gentle swaying. Mireille is waiting for me near Carré Saint-Louis but I land on Mount Royal, unable to correct my angle of descent. I put on my skis so as to meet up with her more quickly. The snow was never more beautiful, nor my body so supple, curving gracefully through the air with ethereal ease, floating upon the joy of being with her again. But she is no longer there. I want to phone her but I cannot remember whom she is living with. I absolutely must not get the name wrong because she would know I am with the woman with whom she is not. "But your embarrassement is stupid," thunders the judge, "since *you* know whom you're with!" But of course, how very simple, indeed: I fly into Philippe's arms and together we enter our comfortable house.

The mouldy house suddenly collapsed, the four walls tumbling outwards, the roof blown away as if a bomb had exploded, letting the sun reach all the rotten, vermin-ridden nooks and crannies. All that's left is a pile of debris in an appalling, wonderful light.

I contemplate the rubble with a feeling of satisfaction mixed with guilt. A police officer approaches and accuses me of having blown up the house. All night long the children and I, wielding pots, bailed out the basement overflowing with stinking sewage water. Then Philippe sent us an electric pump in his private plane, with complete directions for use, but I haven't time to read them with the water rising so fast, stalling the electric train and sweeping away the little remote control airplanes floating among the half-drowned pictures of naked girls. The water is rising so fast now that we cannot hold out: I am afraid the children will drown and I send them upstairs while I stay in the stairway, crying. Philippe arrives like a whirlwind, looks for his already submerged pump, recovers his drifting toys, stirs up great eddies, and shouts "Stop crying, you're making the water rise."

I spot the pump beside a pond. My eldest son is walking along over by the horizon. The second, sitting by the pond, looking worried, is hitting the water with a fishing rod. My daughter runs up, is going to drown, I try to go to her but cannot move: both my feet are muck stuck. I shout as loud as I can, "No! Don't go there!" Her brother sees her and flies into her arms. They are crying. "Mommy's on the bottom." Whereas I am sitting on the edge of the bed, in the hospital. My legs and heart flutter hesitantly, I know not where to step. Leaving this bed is my first step: where can I step without tripping? The floor is covered with jagged blades of broken glass; before you even start walking, a single step means a wound. But the bed is beginning to float and my son raises sails made from sheets. We are going to visit my daughter who lives in a house on stilts. The glass floor reveals a clear spring beneath. I recognize the dance floor in San José Purura where I am dancing with Philippe while fearing the glass will not bear our weight. "Your fear is ludicrous " says Philippe, "you're as light as a feather."

"But what about you? Look, the floor's cracking, your shoes are already wet." The full curve of his fat belly prevents him from seeing the tip of his shoes. I realize with dread that he's expecting a baby, and I reproach him for not having warned me. He assures me he knew nothing about it himself. We go to the dining room where he eats like Gargantua, you can see him bloating up, overflowing his chair. He's going to burst. I flee before the bomb hidden in his clothing explodes, and I sound the alert. The maître d' scolds me and tells me to quit acting like a child. I peer into the dining room where a very slender Philippe is dining with his father.

Mireille has dragged me to a cancer detection clinic to undergo a preventive check-up. We exchange our names for numbers and our clothes for white gowns with slit backs. Mireille is holding hers closed with her left hand, and such puritanism adds to my irritation at having let myself be brought here. "I don't see why you're hiding your bum since that's the very thing you've come here to show." She does not understand my annoyment which stems from embarrassment and disgust. Women are lined up like cattle. "We look like cows, sacred cows, but cows nonetheless." The stench of formaldehyde seeps insidiously from jars full of floating fetuses. I feel terribly sick to the stomach. A woman wearing white hangs numbers around our necks: five around Mireille's, six around mine. We shall be in the same freight car. The woman shouts our numbers, leads us off to be weighed and pushes us towards stalls bearing our numbers, where she makes me lie down and put my feet in stirrups placed high on either side of the stretcher, then she shines a reflector onto my buttocks. The veterinarians come one after the other, each touching his specialty, breasts, abdomen, then they thrust their fingers into me, squeezing me painfully and, deep within my stomach, tearing off a sample representing my category. Then a chariot transports me to a pen where two rows of soldiers are waiting, pointing huge syringes. The row on the left is standing beneath a large sign bearing the word *sterilization*, and the one on the right under another which reads *insemination*. Several people precede me and all give the same answers: "Female, German, Jewish." I am pushed behind them. Where are my papers? I absolutely must identify myself to avoid execution. There ensues a long mad rush through different churches and offices to collect the salvatory documents that I can finally show to the sergeant. He reads aloud: "Female, Québécoise, Catholic.... You are condemned," he tells me, "condemned thrice over." My mother and grandmother are waiting for me in the group of women and are getting impatient because I am taking so long. My daughter comes from the other side, she is going to recognize me and will be taken away in her turn; I must disappear to save her. I flee. The soldiers abandon the prisoners to pursue me through the fences and swamps in a frightful chase that brings me back to my starting point where there is no one left but my mother who is preparing baby bottles while my daughter cradles her child.

    My daughter will soon be giving birth and I have not got anything ready to welcome the child whose arrival I greatly apprehend, for my daughter is frightfully big. Her almost childish head, above this enormous stomach, makes her look as grotesque as would circus mirrors, but she seems unaware of her abnormal state. So as not to destroy her obvious joy, I conspiciously act the part of the good grandmother, but am ever more terrified of what she is carrying. One night, during her sleep, I have a doctor come to open her belly and examine this disturbing fetus. "A photograph will suffice," he tells me.

Developed and printed, the picture is exhibited in a museum. People look at it with indifference: can they possibly see what I see without screaming? *Possible it is, since they don't.* Their indifference astounds me but is a comfort too, protecting me from their indiscretion. Standing not far from the portrait, a man is surrounded by people congratulating him, but he seems absolutely bored. He approaches me and introduces himself: "I am *Quarterman*, the author of the collage you are looking at so attentively."

"I am its mother," I answer.

"Then I'll give it to you." I find it perfectly natural that he should return what he took from me, and I take the portrait home where I can examine it at leisure. A life-sized picture of my daughter, and in her belly three women, like her, are standing, every part of their bodies integrated with hers, each woman smaller and less dressed than the one behind her. The last one, the one in the middle, is very tiny and completely naked, her breasts and pubis clearly visible, with a pretty navel in the middle of her round stomach. I easily recognize my grandmother in this little woman, then, behind her, my mother, and finally me, all three enveloped and carried by my daughter. How will she deliver such a bloodline without dying? Then I take my mother and my grandmother in my arms and try to take them out of her. We are joined together by a long cord that I coil around my throat, risking strangulation, reassured nonetheless by its solid grip.

My daughter puts her arms around my neck and begs me not to leave. I tell her I must, and that if she suffocates me, she too will suffocate. Her arms unravel like a scarf of silken fingers. Then the ground starts rumbling and a terrible storm beats down on the forest, which I flee. At its edge, I look back and see my daughter sleeping peacefully under a glass bell, like the princess in the woods. A fairy comes up and invents a marvellous story in which children are born from sunbeams and have only the moon for mother.

I am stretched out at the centre of the round, warm world as though it were a fluffy cloud, in a blissful state of weightlessness. I am floating like a balloon, free of useless attachments, in a sort of generous futility. From this central sky I can see human heads stuck upside down in the earth's crust, with feet sticking out and beating the air like metronomes. Over the entire surface of the globe, this strange ballet of hairy legs perfectly synchronized in identical movements like teeter-totters, like prancing, like running. As if to compensate for all this apparently useless agitation, I cross my legs like a Buddha and place my hands on my knees. All the heads turn towards me, all identical, with the same exorbitant eyes, the same tight-lipped mouth with false teeth, the same whitened hair hung like rags on nearly bald heads. I see the features of someone I loved, but whom

I refuse to recognize in this ghastly caricature. The multiple head laughs as though to signify that it is really her, and the echo of this sharp, sardonic laugh strikes the inside of the shelter in millions of darts that ricochet onto me. Any moment now this pointed laugh is going to make the earth explode from within. "And why shouldn't the earth explode?" says the forked tongue, "it has to explode so that I can reach your sky."

The fire is burning in the hearth, and Mireille is lying in front of it, on her stomach, knees bent, swinging her legs before the flames. I am sitting on a cushion just beside her, motionless, anxious. Then the same grey head enters, kneels, takes Mireille's legs and wraps them around its neck. Mireille goes on talking to me while the other voraciously sucks at her from the waist to the toes. "You're going to be eaten up," I tell her. She answers, "That's impossible, since you are here." The grey spider then puts its legs on Mireille's heart and sucks it up all at once, like flaccid marrow. A man enters and asks me to give blood for a wounded person who needs a transfusion. He takes my arm and pokes it several times without a drop of blood coming out. He pushes me away and shouts, horrified, "But you have no heart! How can you live?" I look into my chest and see, where the heart should be, an enormous spider. I tell the man to bleed the beast since my blood is there and I am the wounded person he wants to tend. He lies down on me, penetrates me deeply and, having injected his blood into me, disappears in a cloud of smoke. My daughter is sleeping in me as though at the centre of Earth, but already hands are touching her, heads observing her and when I try to protect her against those hands, those heads, I receive great blows in the pit of my stomach. Then she comes out of me and asks me where I'm going. Whereas I am not budging, for fear she will follow me. Philippe, at that very moment, passes by in a race-car going full speed.

While still on the doorstep of the house I realize burglars have come: the big philodendron in the foyer has been knocked over, the black soil spilled onto the green carpet, the paintings knocked awry, the curtains unhooked, the armchairs overturned. Even greater disorder reigns throughout the house, where vandals seem to have held a convention *cum* free-for-all. The upstairs bedrooms are empty of furniture but countless objects litter the floors: broken bottles, cigarette stubs, twisted records, eviscerated books. My son is sitting in a corner, his cat in his lap. I ask him what is happening. "We are moving," he answers. Men dressed in black, heads hooded, enter in procession, take the paintings, and throw them out the window into the courtyard. A great noise of things breaking covers my voice. "Why don't you say anything?" asks my son. I fall silent then, and sit down by him. In the train carrying us both away, he asks me where we are going. I do not know, and his question worries me. "The main thing was to flee," I tell him, "the Inquisition forced me to swear an oath." At the border, they ask us for our I.D. I have none, but I look for some nonetheless, when a woman approaches, stares at me and tells the customs officer, "I know her." I do not know if her revelations are going to condemn or save me. Under what disguise did she know me, when, and in what circumstances? All alone, I am acting in a play involving several characters all of whose roles I am playing, and I am also in the auditorium as director. But I cannot manage to direct the action of my multi-faceted character in a logical fashion. Cut out, eliminate, reduce! shouts a voice. I am quite at a loss as to which of these characters I should liquidate; none of them is entirely satisfying on its own, but it seems to me that their number gives a certain density to the production. Yet the voice is right, the whole thing is too cluttered, and so lacks unity. I wish the voice would whisper to me the cuts to make, that it would help me to eliminate the less representative characters, some of which may even be quite useless. Can the little girl climbing the tree be on stage at the same time as the suckling mother and the young girl studying diligently and the one making love in different places? This play is like a circus with different activities going on simultaneously. In the lions' cage I must confront at least thirty hairy and feathered beasts, wild and domesticated, which I am really having trouble holding in check. These animals were not made to get along together and I shall not long be able to keep them under control. Who can I blame? The manager who offered me this position, or myself, who so rashly accepted it? I decide to resign. The manager protests, but I make him recognize my rights to a retirement pension, since I have been practising this crazy profession for forty years. "In that case," grants the manager, "you may leave, but the animals belong to you." They all obediently let themselves be captured. I drop them into a pretty little inkwell and I put it in my pocket.

    I have been standing in this spot for so long that the ground has softened beneath my feet and I am sinking more and more. Soon, if I do not move, I shall go under for good, but how to get out, and where to go? I see holes behind me, holes I got out of since I recognize my dried tracks. Am I going to move again just so as to go on walking and making more holes? Why not stall here, in this filled-in hole? Around, roads lead off in various directions but I do not want to ask them where they lead. Fatigue, passiveness hold me back and will swallow me up if I do not make the effort to walk some more. I am looking for a downhill road on which to roll my fatigue and let it go tumbling down, but space suddenly folds up around me into a funnel with very smooth sides. Into it someone is pouring a treacherous liquid that will put me to sleep if I drink it. Despite my burning thirst, I keep my mouth closed and the lukewarm liquid glides over my face, runs along my body and soaks the ground into which I am still sinking. I have drunk too much, I am drunk, the sails of the walls are rocking my bedroom, I am on a floating island, one of the Philippines. The water from his hands, his mouth, his genitals caresses me everywhere, between my legs, my breasts, under my armpits, my neck, my cheeks. I drink it, I become intoxicated with him, I am sinking in a lukewarm, salty sea, slowly, slowly, under Philippe's gentle pressure. Suddenly the descent becomes extremely fast, hands and feet bound I sink straight down into black, icy water. I beg Philippe to open the wardrobe, I am already nearly asphyxiated. "I'll give you artificial respiration," mocks Philippe on the other side of the door. The pearl necklace he gave me is hanging on a clotheshanger and open oysters are biting my toes. I eat the pearls and cover myself with scales. Philippe opens the refrigerator, takes out a dozen Malpeque Bay oysters, opens them, stares, and in a rage throws them into the garbage. I remind him that one must dive to find pearls, or else cultivate them. "You can also buy them," he retorts. I rush out of the kitchen and go vomit all the pearls into the toilet, they roll through the sewers, descend the river and recover their brilliance as soon as they reach the sea. I am angrily vacuuming when the telephone rings. My mother is telling me of the joys of the past as of happiness that I had forgotten to experience. "You are still young," she says, "you'll see that being sixty isn't funny at all." Great sadness oppresses me as though the worst were yet to come. I again pick up the loathsome vacuum by the end of its cold, crooked spine holding a soft belly packed with dust and connected to a long, sinuous grey cord. Filthy machine voraciously sucking up filth! Fuming, I snatch out the cord. At once the stomach subsides, flattens, collapses onto its microbes. A vast silence accompanies the death of the monster, which gets a violent kick. The bag explodes in a stinking cloud whose fatal fallout surrounds the beast's head, covering it almost totally. "And here is the aging couple," declares the guide, showing the handle, slightly curved at its end and whose base is thrust into the greyish entrails lying on the carpet. "Man is dust and to dust shall he return." I protest: "This couple isn't dead, nothing is lost, nothing created, and here, sir, is their child." With him looking on I operate a portable battery-powered vacuum cleaner which in one gulp wolfs down the pile of scattered entrails. All is clean once more, and I can rock my son: "You are a good baby, a good little baby, clean as can be." When it is time to put him to bed, I cannot get down from the rocking chair balanced on the fourth rung of a ladder. The chair topples over and I save my son by hanging on to a post. Philippe enters and, without noticing my bizarre position, sits down and rocks himself in the chair. I ask him if he has brought the medication prescribed by the doctor. "I haven't had time to go," he answers.

"Have you repaired the ladder?"

"But I can't do everything," he protests. That is so obvious that I wonder how I could have asked him such a silly question. But the fire has already reached all the rooms in the house and the flying firemen let a ladder down from the sky; I climb quickly up, while Philippe goes on sleeping, heedless of the inferno. I arrive late at Mr. Tinelli's class in moral philosophy: "The scale of values proposed by theologians respects freedom..." I have trouble hearing the rest and am most unhappy not to receive the precious teachings. I start crying, and the nurse consoles me by announcing that the operation was a success. She takes the cotton out of my ears and, enraptured, I can finally listen to silence.

There are Mireille, the sea, the summer day, very handsome young friends. Happiness fixed in a perfect, luminous moment, each being, each thing holding a privileged place. I would like to die of active contemplation, dissolve into the blue of the sky, *be* this dizzylingly deep blue, this realm of absolute gentleness and purity. My body lightens and glides in this blue cold as steel, yet softer than milk. I am swimming in the sea, I dive, I surface, I split the water at incredible speed, I am a dolphin, I am the water, the sun, life, it's everywhere around me, in me, immensely happy am I. On the beach Mireille is speaking and her words stick to my limbs like jellyfish: "Look how voraciously she is seizing the sea, watch out! Watch out! She's going to swallow it all!" The sea dries up at once, and I remain glued to its muddy bottom like a crab. I angrily crawl towards the beach which towers up three tiers of cliffs. "Aha, here are my three enemies, only three, that's not much, I can surmount them." I climb the three cliffs with the ease of a young she-goat, up to the great disappointment of the peak, which is only a minute platform just big enough to hold a crotchet rest. This ridiculous rest area is clinging to the base of another three-storied mountain. A seagull with huge wings is sitting on eggs near me. When it flies off, I take an egg and shut myself into it. The shell is big, I have all the room I need to do nothing, but as I have feathers on my wings, I write a message to give to the homing pigeon: "S.O.S.: three enemies ahoy: God, other people, and me." A bit of shell falls away and I stick my head out the hole: the flood is not over. I close the window and spend years trying to draw a dove. Just as I am finishing it, Philippe takes it and locks it up in a cage while I fly out the window.

Mireille and I are visiting my grandmother who,

despite her paralysis, still laughs, always laughs, and talks to me about the time when I was "a real pest, but really sweet." "Are you good now?" On seeing my bicycle she is scandalized: "You! A married woman, riding a bicycle!" She would not have been more indignant had I mounted a lover. I take the bicycle out of the kitchen while grandmother goes on talking to Mireille as though she were me, not realizing her error. She is scolding her, and I find that very funny. Leaning against the doorpost, I watch Mireille living in my stead and see in that no drawbacks, but rather happiness. However, when Mireille plays along too well and answers with idiocies, I am at first uncomfortable, then peeved. On the road I ask her "But who's who?" She takes my hand but my anger does not abate. We still have two other hands with which to fight, and we use them.

    She flees and I keep working at my sculpture, a reproduction of the Venus of Milo. Philippe asks me why I am not giving her arms. "Because this way it's easier to transport," say I. I take the statue and go put it to bed. "Hug me tight," begs Philippe, "tear my back, scratch me, ride my back." My arms are motionless, hard as marble and just as cold. Philippe, shocked, quickly rises, goes down to the basement and busies himself with wires, metal, a motor. He builds a highly sophisticated robot which he operates with a battery in his pocket. The steel arms are jointed like lobsters' and slice the air in big jerky sweeps. A door slides open and reveals the monster's abdomen where thousands of razor blades are hopping in several voracious, threatening rows. Arms and stomach open, the robot approaches Philippe who thrusts a long beam into its fangs. The little saws work so well that the sawdust is as fine as blond sand. At the same time the robot disintegrates, and Philippe becomes so terrifyingly angry that his stomach bursts. Lying down he looks at me, his eyes like darts, then rings the bell hanging on the bedstead. A red-haired woman with bright red lips approaches him and bows her head over his belly. I turn away and hear frightful moans. I run to my room where I find long red hair in my bed.

Snow, lake, cemetery, sky and cold are blue except for a little spot, out there in the field, black and teeming, unpleasant in this perfect polar transparence. People have formed a circle around grandmother's tomb. A priest sprinkles holy water which immediately freezes from the aspergillum to the ground in a dazzling rainbow. It is all very beautiful and I have no wish to cry on this day of grandmother's snowial. The others do, and their tears freeze in icicles on their faces. In a few moments the massed relatives freeze into a block of ice. My daughter gives me kicks in the stomach, impatient to get out. I am against it, it is too cold to bring her into the world, the storm is raging outside and Philippe claims it is not weather to go out in and that I can easily give birth in the house since childbirth is not an illness. We scream so loud all us women together that the judge threatens to have the room cleared. Silence! Silence! They gag us one after the other but the shouts, rather than stopping, increase and even cover the pealing bells. The terrified priests, holding their aspergillums, move among the women: "They are possessed!

How can they still shout when they've been gagged?" The women then get up all together and reveal hundreds of newborns on the flagstones, screaming to split your eardrums. As the first reporter on the spot, I try to question the women, who remain silent. A man snatches my notebook and throws it away, insulting me. "Balderdash! Balderdash!" A snake comes out of the font and swallows the aspergillum. I shout "Miracle," the women kneel, the shouts cease and the priest climbs up to the pulpit, a pulpit so sad and fragile that it tumbles under his weight to the great mirth of the Holy Innocents who enter a mock battle armed with aspergillum tomahawks. The mommies start shouting again. I hasten to write my article and give my will to the lawyer.

In this hell, I know everyone. In such good company I should feel happy, but on the contrary I am disappointed that hell is not what I expected. Philippe approaches and asks "But how did you imagine the place?" I cannot manage to describe the hell I dreamt of, and Philippe, taking advantage of my hesitation, tries to sell me on this hell: "You've got everything, you can cook, have your friends in, sleep when you like. Look, there's our room." A young woman is lying in the bed, naked, asleep. I flee into an office where a hoary lawyer with a patriarch's beard greets me kindly, albeit I repeat to him a single sentence - "I want to leave." "Come, my child, it is not a paradise but after all you must learn to appreciate things, not be too choosy, men are weak and you cannot demand of them a hell beyond their reach." Children are having fun fighting in a room next door; elsewhere,

I see a table loaded with exquisite dishes before obese guests, women trying on clothing that is too small. Philippe makes his train go off the tracks, a worker gets his finger squashed, a mother rocks an eyeless child. I try to leave but Philippe smashes his fist on the table and screams "I love you! You shall not leave." We enter our room where I see the young girl stretched out, her mouth and nose torn off, holding Philippe's penis in her hand. He covers her with a sheet, lays me down beside her and envelops me in his arms.

I cannot recognize any former classmates at this alumni reunion, and am wondering if it was really my class that was summoned. Seated near the door, in a church pew, I feel uncomfortable and would like to leave without being noticed. The little room is half dark, and I seek some face I know so as not to seem an intruder, so as not to confess my mistake, and to mask the unbearable feeling of being one too many. A friend I have not seen for ages approaches me, stares lengthily deep into my eyes with a brazen, searching gaze, and invites me to dance. No one is dancing, and a hundred thousand eyes are watching us. Yet I follow her. She is guiding me awkwardly, we are disastrously ridiculous, and I tell her, "You can see that it's simply impossible!" She laughs and shows me the cast on her leg. I help her sit down and put her crutches beside her. Mireille approaches, sits down without a word to us and removes the prothesis that was paralyzing my left hand. We are still silent. I want to leave and I do not want to: I feel so fine. The silver disk of a powerful reflector encircles two very tall, beautiful women, tenderly embracing, who seem to dance but almost without moving. Their hands glide on shoulders, backs, hips, uncoiling liquid caresses that make them undulate like sea algae. Noses glued to the aquarium, a crowd of bystanders is watching these strange, graceful creatures. A man is talking to his son about sea horses, while another explains that these mermaids are a marvelous tourist attraction. Philippe seems to be greatly enjoying this night club and is watching the swimmers, his eyes moist with longing. My curiosity is as great as his, but it wanders from him to them, interested both by the show itself and by its troubling effect on Philippe who suddenly dives into the pool. And I am splashed. The lake water is ice cold and I run out to lie in the sun. I am cold. Mireille approaches, covers me with her blue overcoat and looks at me in blue, in green, in emerald. I fall asleep on the brim of her eyelids, between sea and sky.

Somewhere, in an unfamiliar city, I am walking aimlessly, smiling, among many people. A man approaches and informs me, "Don't you know, you're expected." I do not understand. "I see," says the man. "You are too learned to understand such simple things." I shrug and inform him that I prefer to be alone. "No doubt," he retorts, "but that's easier as a twosome." I continue walking on the beach where children are playing with colored blocks of different shapes that fit into each other. Mireille is sitting among them, digging in the sand. I ask her what she is doing. "I'm looking for a disinterested act," she answers, showing her hand attached to several others, some holding her back and others pushing her towards me. I find that hand monstrous and she hastens to offer me the other, which is perfectly normal. I cannot reach it because I am playing the piano and my mother is checking my scales. I am wearing a brown skirt and a yellow blouse; my mother tells me to smile for the picture she is taking. I would like very much to cry because I am afraid she will see my dirty shoes. I flee and the nun scolds me because my skirt is too short, shorter even than my braids. She lets down my hair, brushes it and spreads it out around me. It covers me to the ankles, revealing my dirty shoes. Then I climb a tree so as to no longer stain my shoes, which I hang on a branch. A bird immediately comes to rest in them. It is already night, but I wish neither to disturb the bird nor to go home barefoot. Mireille joins me, bringing my brother's clothing. I climb down the tree and go home in my brother's stead.

I am serene in this house, seated by the window, looking at the lake, when the plaster lion on the chest of drawers opens its mouth, a huge, red mouth. I turn away from such horror and my eyes meet, on a shelf, the head of a Negress with real earrings in her ears and, on her head, a real gold plate for carrying real fruit made of real wax. Lions, Blacks, Africa, where am I? Two lamps light up, two Chinese figurines contorted so as to carry on their shoulders green lamp shades from which balls of black fluff are hanging. This light reveals other objects: wax flowers planted in a sort of blue boat, a bleeding Sacred Heart over the door, three bound books stuck for all eternity between lead book-shaped molds, and countless exotic landscapes cut out of calendars. I rise and enter an entirely white room with no furniture, save a kneeling stool: it is undoubtedly a cell in a monastery. The door opens and a missionary introduces me to his converts: I discover, in rank, the lion, the Negress, the Chinese women. I am going to die of chagrin and the whole community gathers to attend my edifying end. Then I sit on my bed and shout that I have lost my faith. The mother superior thinks I am delirious and dismisses all the nuns, who kneel in the corridor and sing psalms. Two nurses are holding me down and trying to prevent me from shouting, they sprinkle holy water on me to exorcize my scandalous mortal agony. I want to leave, not die here. Philippe arrives in an ambulance. I jump in the truck amidst chairs, boxes, tables, but immediately ask Philippe to let me off because I no longer want to move. The truck keeps speeding along and I throw furniture out all along the way. We run out of gas in the middle of the desert. Philippe has disappeared but a lion's mouth is laughing redly before me. I light fires to warm myself. Camels pass by. They look haughty, pretentious and inane, but this parade fascinates me. Mummy tells me that if I am really good, she will buy me a plaster camel. I cry because I want a real camel. When Philippe invites me to accompany him to Morocco, I find the idea bizarre. Why Morocco? "Because of the camels," he answers me. I cannot grasp what he means, and let him leave with a caravan while I walk alone towards the sea.

   It has been raining so much and so long that the house is only an island in the middle of a lake. Fog completes our total isolation. I want to land somewhere, to be welcomed, dried, warmed. I see a telephone in the booth but I do not know whom to call: have not those I love all perished in this deluge? And long ago, since we were all in the same bottomless boat? My raft is floating in the dark, shadows move in the water, and sharks' snouts come and lean, patient and sniggering, on the rubber edge. I am not afraid, but I feel the strange need to tell someone so. A little to the left I see a friend standing on a slowly sinking castle. She asks me to join her. "It's not much fun," she says, "but the house is solid." I greatly hesitate to accept this job offer but the big desk, even if it seems to me to be sinking, comforts me and I am happy to see it even if I hesitate to disembark. Philippe asks me if I have found work. "I cannot support you for doing nothing," he says, "you and the children have been sucking at me for fifteen years." My statue sinks straight down and together we watch it descend from the sky. The raft is beginning to leak and I am angry at Philippe for not fixing it. He tells me, "Put your finger in the hole, it's much simpler."

"We're going to drown!"

"Not at all," he reassures me. He is already up to his neck in water but does not seem to notice. I see children hanging from clouds and who are going to fall into the sea with all this water endlessly bursting forth. I finally manage to reach Mireille on the telephone. She tells me that the mist is the soul's underground and that we must beware the sun, which is swallowing us up. An insanc storm cuts us off. Locked up in my lunar module body I am floating, waiting for someone to free me through the portholes. I am back from the moon, and the frogmen get bogged down in the simple manoeuvres required to slide the bolts so as to open the hatches. My fear of staying locked up in there, suffocated by men's awkwardness, is so great that I decide to leave by the door and walk on the water.

In a big asphalt field diverse people are grouped under various banners on which I can read, Singles Here, Wives Here, Lovers Here, Lesbians Here, Nuns Here, Prostitutes Here, Intellectuals Here, Sportswomen Here. Each group is peacefully grazing beneath its distinctive banner. At the entrance, a bulldog in charge of keeping order asks me for my ticket so as to direct me to my seat. So I take out a parchment bearing the word *Woman* in beautiful gilt lettres, with the "W" illuminated, as in ancient manuscripts. The man wants to seize it, but I stop him. It is a sacred book: only priestesses have the right to touch it. I withdraw into a large park to read the book which contains no word save *Woman* written at the top of each page of fine, white paper. This reading plunges me into a kind of ecstasy, body and soul cuddled together within a pleasant warmth. When I finish writing this page of my journal, the notebook is finished and I go to put it away in the chest with the other nine, which I find scattered, torn. Someone has stolen my soul! Distraught, angry, hurt, I run through the house, the town, everywhere, seeking the guilty party. A group of people blocks the road and I recognize the pages of my notebooks brandished by hilarious, threatening gorillas dancing around a bonfire. The jungle is thick, suffocating, I want to get out but I am just a little girl, and all alone

I shall never be able to reach that castle at the mountain top. I ask an old woman to help me. She gives me a parcel that has been left for me: it is the nine notebooks of my journal. "There's one missing," I tell her. "You'll find it in the castle." Descending the stairs, I meet Philippe who asks me where I am going. "I'm off to look for myself," I tell him. I recognize the road passing above the houses I have lived in, beautiful, pleasant houses, tempting, where I would like to stop and settle in again and perhaps, finally, rest; but a great wind is pushing me out to sea where words are floating like wrecks. I name them and they at once sink straight down. Now the surface is calm, polished like a mirror, anonymous, bluishly transparent. A ship passes by and a sailor asks who I am. I cannot tell him: to name myself would be to sink, hands and feet bound, body in a chest. "My name is in the last notebook," I tell him. I enter the castle and find the notebook on the table, a blank notebook in which I must write thousands of sentences to successfully inscribe my name.

It is snowing heavily, fine, dense, infinite, melding sky and earth into the same white wall erected just beside me. I am walking on snowshoes through the forest and listening to the spruce sagging under the weight of the snow. Silence, save this discreet noise in a nearby infinity drawn round me in tender intimacy. I am tempted to lie down here in the soft snow, close my eyes, go to sleep, accept this invitation to die of tenderness. When the farmer comes to plow, the soil is opened, upturned, but I do not really awaken. I lie dormant, waiting for the infinite "yes" of ripe wheat deep within me. Softly, the doctor's voice informs me I have a daughter. A man of the cloth, behind a window, takes the child and performs a strange ritual: "Unclean, thrice unclean, woman, may the devil leave thee," while he pours things into her mouth, onto her head and smears her body with little crosses. Convinced I have brought a monster into the world, I scream with despair while everyone seems to find the situation perfectly normal. "She is being purified," they say. Woman, unclean, greedy, sinful belly. In a rage I hurl fruit at my brother who has just launched an assault on the apple tree I have climbed. He picks up the apples falling around him, puts them in a canon and subjects me to heavy shelling that leaves my tree leafless but me unharmed. The war ends due to lack of ammunition, and we are sitting in the grass looking for another game. My mother is calling us, but he puts his fingers in my ears so I cannot hear. Mother comes and asks what we are doing. My brother explains that I fell from the tree and he is consoling me. Then the neighbour forbids her children to play with us because we are perverts. All my pupils are watching me while the headmistress gives me the lesson plan for the class in Religion: "We must restore the sense of sin in children." I begin: "Look, it's winter. The trees are leafless, that's why Adam was born in the summer." The headmistress kicks me out of kindergarten. I tell my brother, who is Pharaoh of Egypt, what has just happened. He laughs a lot and asks me the name of the strange county I come from. I cannot remember. He scolds me and tells me it is shameful to have forgotten I am of royal lineage, a direct descendant of the Ramses dynasty. "Ramses?" interrupts Philippe, who guffaws, "you know Ramses doesn't make babies." My brother the King condemns Philippe to sterility and I immediately give birth to a child beautiful as the sun.

I have to cross this room and that simple procedure seems like torture to me. I am afraid of falling, slipping, staggering, zigzagging, stumbling. Philippe tells me, "Lets go to bed, you're drunk." He has given me seven glasses but I have knocked them all over, accidentally, ashamed of my awkwardness in front of all these people. Yet I must leave, but I cannot make myself do it, I am so afraid I'll tumble head over heels, for what pressing reason I do not know. I take little steps forward on the verge of my clumsiness in front of all these people who are wearing glasses as though to better see how awkward I am. My uneasiness grows so much I must stop. Then someone approaches me and I see a horrible head: his thick glasses are grafted directly on to the lobes of his brain and replace his eyes. "How can you see like that?" I ask him.

"What counts is that I see," he answers, "but why are you naked?" I am wearing a long dress and sandals.

"Get up," orders someone else.

"But I am not seated!" The fabricated eyes are still looking at me but I know they cannot see me, so I can walk without fear since no one will know. Then Philippe shouts "Watch out, you're going to fall into the well! Wait for me to bring your glasses." He puts glasses on my nose and a huge chasm plunges in front of me. I turn towards

Philippe whose two-faced head is wearing two pairs of glasses. The telephone rings and I rush to answer. The optometrist informs me my glasses are ready and that I can stop in to pick them up tonight. I go back to bed, it is dark, very dark, but I know it is dark because my optometrist told me so, while holding my glasses. Philippe comes in and stumbles against the shut door. "It is three in the morning," I say, "the office is closed." While he goes to sleep in the bedroom next door I read my body with my fingertips and find that its story is beautiful.

A little girl is moaning in the yard, "Mommy, come and help me, Mommy come and help me," endlessly but without conviction, it is like a hesitant call already stuck in soft pleasure. From my room I can neither see the yard nor go down there. They fall in the snow, the man's voice is triumphant, the little girl softly cries hoarse sobs wrenched from her woman's body. A stranger enters my hotel room and possesses me as simply as though he were drinking a cup of tea, then goes off to the beach. I am amazed the snow has melted so fast and I watch the bathers with great pleasure: such grace in the water, this ease of freed bodies. All I have to do is soar off on my tiptoes, and I fly over the bathers like a seagull, light, borne by the sole joy of my body. The confessor sternly scolds me and reminds me it is forbidden to be light-fingered. I try to explain that I am not light-fingered, but feathered, a bird. "Of prey, of prey," that's it exactly. He looks like a crow and when he leans over my daughter his long black wings entirely cover her. I have a solid grip on the rifle but I am afraid to shoot for fear of killing her too. The revolution is raging all around and bombs are bursting everywhere, the sky is afire. "It is the end of the world," shrieks the crow. The good news goes round the world, the ruckus suddenly stops and in a green pasture quivering with daisies young people are dancing, strolling, having fun, happy. Off to one side I tirelessly dig a hole in the park. "I am a gravedigger," I tell the young man who has approached and who goes off again with a shrug. But to Philippe, who is looking at the little mound in our yard, I proudly announce that I have planted a tree, some flower seeds. It is snowing heavily and I plant a cross in the frozen garden. "It's a stake," I say. I wait for flowers to cover the cross.

The fortune-teller is asking me to open my hand up wide but I cannot because, even open, my hand is never wide enough. I keep my fist tightly closed as though I were hiding something in it. "Open it up, open it up, show me what's there." My hands open, and are empty. "I've lost it," I tell her. In a great forest planted with beautiful trees, I am seeking what I lost, and at the same time picking marsh marigolds. Soon my arms are so full I cannot see where I am going. The flowers give off a syrupy smell that makes me sick to the stomach. My mother cannot understand how such a beautiful bouquet can make me sick, but since she is on the other side of the wall I cannot give her this bouquet which seems to please her so much. I throw all the flowers away and continue looking for some other unfindable thing here. Hellebores sprout shoots everywhere and grow, monstrously smothering, enveloping, in wide, intertwined, sticky leaves that bend over me and pour forth an unbearable scent. I am suffering the ghastly experience of being embalmed without being dead. My clenched, cold hands fiercely claw at the soil above me: I will reach the sun, I will reach the sun. I see the soles of human feet beginning to take root. Their weight becomes unbearable and my ditch starts shaking. I crawl, vile caterpillar, I crawl, I climb up the rough bark, I eat all the leaves on the tree and shut myself up in a cocoon. The wrappings are still holding me tight to the tree, but high, high in the sky. My dazzling wings finally burst free into the light and, filled with emotion, I fly off towards a perfumed mauve.

Never have I been given so lovely a present: the cubes, of diverse materials and every size, have an infinite variety of shades of color, from the brightest, greedy red to a yellow splashing with sun. I am sitting in the midst of these delightful pieces, all so desirable that I cannot make up my mind which one to choose. I choose an orange one and just as I am about to grasp it I get a rap on the knuckles. "So you haven't learned your lesson yet, you stubborn little thing?" The woman is as curt as a telephone pole, and just as grey. She terrifies me, I would like to flee but the pretty blocks surround me like a wall of wonderful dreams that I could not cross through without breakage. Why won't she just let me play in peace and quiet? I forget she is there and my hand reaches out again, this time getting painfully burned. "Repeat after me," says the pole, "It is very ugly, I know it is, I want it." Sin is defined in its three fatal dimensions and I am astonished that these beautiful, square, many-colored certitudes should be so fatal. I go and sulk in a desolate region bristling with rocks, crushed with heat, where I am dying of thirst. Philippe brings me a magnificent rose with pearls of water in its corolla. "Yes, I want it," I tell the witnessing priest. I eagerly embrace the rose, I drink it, refreshing myself, while its stem keeps getting longer, slides along my abdomen then pierces me deep in the belly. My blood flows along my thighs, burning blood from a scarlet wound. I must cross through a great crowd and my blood, like a curse, will not stop flowing, to my great shame. Arrows are shot from everywhere and one of them hits me just between the ribs. More blood flows, I am getting exhausted, I must lie down, my head on her stomach, a very long, infinitely long curve warm beneath my cheek like another cheek, that quivering cheek of her secret face, her belly that accepts love and nurtures it, since I can hear the child whispering in my ear what a tender welcome it received. "Let's drink to the child's health," says Mireille. A castle of pretty ice cubes is melting in a martini. The olive has silver antennae and a scarlet mouth. "We have too many guests," I tell Mireille, "I'll never be able to serve so many people. But I stop worrying when I realize that they have all helped themselves and are having fun with blocks of many colours.

   Holidaying with Philippe I am thoroughly bored, when Mireille enters our bedroom and introduces her husband. I was unaware she was married, and this piece of news overjoys me, as though sharing the same nuisance brought us even closer together. The air is hot and muggy, we are drinking Pernod and playing cards like idiots. I walk by the sea and as Mireille is not there I must return to play cards with her. Everyone is waiting for something without knowing what, nor from whom, nor how. I make a fan of my cards and, lying down, I wave it while Mireille's husband makes love to me. "Why are you hiding behind the partition?" asks Mireille who rolls up the blinds and kisses me on the mouth. At that the director flies into a rage and threatens to take away my role. Philippe, the cameraman, shouts about wasting film for nothing, the whole crew is upset. They are waiting for me to finish writing the script and I am paralyzed, unable to find an ending that will satisfy everyone. Normally, it should be tragic, but the producer wants a happy, profitable ending. Mireille, the star I have created, is posing for the photographers on a pile of manuscripts, and I am watching her, the world at the tip of my pencil, arm raised like the Statue of Liberty's. People are climbing up thousands of steps inside me, up into my hand to look at the earth, while I remain frozen, my raised arm getting heavier and heavier, trapped in a final pose. Lord, how exhausting! I shan't be able to stick it out. But how to get down from this gigantic pedestal which is so high it makes me dizzy? And how could I get rid of these tightrope-walking, trapeze artist spiders giving me a stuffy brain? My mother comes in with friends who visit me like a museum, admiring various objects. I leave quickly by the back door and find myself in a big field where I take a leaf from a tree and inscribe on it the word: freedom. "I want something original!" screams the director. I maintain that I've made a real find but Philippe disagrees, he refuses to shoot such stupidity, and I hand in my resignation. But they do not want to release me from my contract. Shirley Temple comes to serve as my lawyer and gives a vibrant presentation on the disastrous psychological consequences of premature commitments. They award her an Oscar. I leave the cinema, disgusted.

Mireille is naked, standing on a dune, her arms along her body, palms turned outwards, bust high, head falling back, blond hair all down her back. People around are admiring her, thinking she's a statue. Women, just like the men, are going on and on about the beauties of her body; and their desires, miraculously cast in bronze, are satisfied on her bust, her shoulders, her stomach, her thighs. Her genitalia are beauty itself, and everyone turns into artists so as to enjoy them. She is sketched, photographed, described, fraudulently taken over. Then the group's psychiatrist rises and announces that there has been enough sublimation for today and that everyone must now go back home to the suburbs. The patients put their work clothes back on: togas, aprons, smocks, soutanes, and slide on all fours into a very dark tunnel. A huge fire is lighting up the night and we are sitting around it: Mireille, the psychiatrist, his wife, some friends. The psychiatrist keeps changing seats without my understanding why, until he comes to sit by me. Suddenly he hugs me and raises my skirt. I get up at once and flee onto the dock, he runs after me, gesticulating and agitated. Suddenly I stumble against a rock and fall flat on my stomach:

he crashes onto me and thrusts into me from behind. I shriek with pain but he shouts even louder, like a madman, his shouts accompanied by great thrusts of his hips. "I'll cure you, take that, I'll cure you, take that"; then he abandons me on the dock, inert, torn, raging with pain and shame. Philippe gets up and brings me a towel and a glass of water. When my strength comes back I crawl towards the shelter of the black tunnel to hide my shame with the others.

I cannot see him but I know he is there, inside, beside, everywhere, he knows me and I love him. I drink him in the spring, I hear him in the trees, I touch him in the coolness of the grass, I smell him in the warm scent of the earth, I am penetrated as by the very air I breathe. I am living in my childhood willow, so tall, so wide that I can place a nest in the cradle of each branch in an oasis ever vibrant with the caresses of my naked hands and feet on its open arms. I tell Mireille about my tree, and she accepts to come and see it. Both of us are standing in front of the magnificent willow but Mireille does not recognize it. My disappointment is immense, as big as the second branch, the one that curves like a hammock and whose hollow I have already filled with dry grass. The tree and I are one and the same, my childhood sleeps in it amidst green dreams, but Mireille is not touched. Lightning cuts the tree in two and I see it stretched out, rigid, its heart stolen by ants, its great body invaded by moss, my joy devastated, crushed. With a heavy heart I am playing the violin in an orchestra giving a concert under the trees before villagers who have suffered from the war. There is a crowd, a stray dog and a German prisoner tied to a stake. My violin strings break one after the other but I go on playing my solo, knowing that the strings are broken, the prisoner's chain is solid, the crowd tired, the dog mean. I am playing with tears in my eyes, aimlessly, just out of habit, because I must play, and from my stringless violin comes a soothing melody, gentle as the breeze in the tree. I abandon the bow, and the music continues: someone is playing my music in my stead, and better, much better than I. I climb my willow and lie down, my cheek against the bark, my eyes full of blue. "You can cut down the tree," I tell the prisoner. The saw plays Haydn's violin concerto in C major, the willow weeps, and so does the German. Then the huge green parachute slowly rises, wrenches itself from the earth, transports me onto a mountain where it immediately takes root. I am unfamiliar with this country and I ask a passer-by where I am. He says, "I had nothing and they came and took it. Now here I am, rich." My tree is overflowing with fruit and I realize the man is right.

    People are coming to deposit, with infinite care, all sorts of boxes in a huge chest with countless drawers. No one can see anyone and everyone seems to be acting clandestinely, as fast as possible, disappearing as soon as the box is in place. Later, the night watchman lowers his fork like a portcullis in front of the chest. Simultaneously a curtain opens from the other side where professors are teaching their courses, each in front of a group of pupils packed tight under a glass globe. A life-size plastic model comes and stands in front of the professors who take from it the parts needed to illustrate their lectures: a doctor takes an abdomen, an anthropologist a jaw, a dietician a stomach; a psychologist measures the length of the nose, a sociologist draws a coordinate in the brain, each of them seizes me, mutilates me, catalogues me, and I cannot protest, for the Great Anaesthetist has condemned me to live in society. Exhausted, I do not get home until the wee hours of the morning. I have left my heart somewhere and it is hurting me terribly. I cannot go to work like this, in bits and pieces, skinned alive, mutilated. But the guard has already raised the portcullis and I deposit my night in a drawer with the others', among hairy little bat-winged beasts. "Belle de jour," the guard tells me, don't fret, I'll return your heart when you leave." From my office I telephone Mireille. Her husband announces they are giving him a heart transplant, and he thanks me for having offered him my heart. Philippe is watching me as though expecting me to die but I smile, reassured, when I see him dining in a restaurant with friends, a big hole in his ribs.

 I am circling a disturbing beast stealthily lying on its belly to mask its real intentions and make people think, by this innocent pose, that it is brooding peace, warm, milky peace within easy reach of mouth. I yearn to lie beneath it, fed, satisfied, protected. To suckle in safety. Philippe asks me to approach but I hesitate because the ground seems muddy and the belly seems to be sinking. It is snowing continuously and the beast alone is giving off a bit of warmth and life amidst the icy death all around. I am cold but upright. Snowflakes race and swirl about me, accelerating madly, whirling into a tornado that swallows me. How everything's spinning! I live, I laugh, I descend, descend, it's mildly intoxicating, and then suddenly I am projected out of the maelstrom like a small, skinned, grated, rounded, smooth ball. My arms no longer move except inside me, my eyes, ears and skin have turned inwards and, astonished, I stare at this strange, inner moonscape. Scattered about are craters like the marks left by projectiles shot by Earth, hard mountains of vertical faith sliced through by ravines, and everywhere grey sand packed into scattered blocks, faces which, even petrified, I can recognize by the trails they have left, luminous furrows outlining, in this wan valley, roads all leading to an abyss. Abyss of the soul, abyss of absence, ab, ab, the volcano is mocking, threatening, boiling: one slip, and I'll tumble in. I look back where I left some bits, gather them up, and try to piece them together, wondering if they are going to hold together or if I shall have to throw these bits, like a thousand well-stacked deaths, into the abyss. The stones keep multiplying and they are everywhere now: some shine, others smell of sulphur, some crumble when I just look at them whereas others, sharp and hard, minute, become embedded in my eyes. I am suffering too much, I want to get out of myself through a little hole in the temple and I reach for the revolver near by.

"Why are you tearing out the flowers?", asks Mireille.

"I'm pulling up the weeds."

"You'll never be able to, there are too many." Then thousands of daisies burst forth all together in a thousand suns. I pick a bouquet and go offer it to my mother who turns her back, bent over faded orchids.

I am leaving this bedroom as though it were the longest winter of my life, perhaps the very winter of my life. My toes play in the warm earth as I transplant eggplants. I feel well, a deep well-being such as only, I think, a woman can feel, with this warmth snuggled deep in my belly and my vast, unspecified desire, a sort of active love for all that lives, is around me and that I may welcome. The sun, the cats, the garden, the peacefulness: one would have to be mad, or ill-mannered, not to worship this instant. And there is the miracle: I *am* worshipping this instant. For the first time lucidity does not wound but cradles me, I greet myself without wanting to spit in my face, I meet me face to face, I commune with myself. My good and my evil reconciled at last, my heart welcoming my arm and hand and all they touch.

My life becomes gentle and tender, reclining within me, finally tamed, and we can love each other without hurting each other. And then, for a moment, I am afraid. Here I am, free as a cat, but the tree with its everyday roots of water and leaf denounces my uprooting. I plunge my feet into the earth, I restate my faith, I glorify my fear, I bless my insecurity.

The children are smiling at me, from afar. Mireille and Philippe have left, back to back, to face one another on the other side of the world.

I remain standing, naked, alone, exposed, vulnerable, I want to risk being myself, to die in my skin. That too must be dignity.